Ghosts Galore

Also edited by Robert Fisher

AMAZING MONSTERS:
Verses to Thrill and Chill

GHOSTS GALORE
Haunting Verse

edited by
ROBERT FISHER

illustrated by Rowena Allen

ff
faber and faber

First published in 1983
by Faber and Faber Limited
3 Queen Square London WC1N 3AU
Printed and bound in Great Britain by
Mackays of Chatham PLC, Chatham, Kent

A CIP record for this book is
available from the British Library

ISBN 0-571-13926-4

2 4 6 8 10 9 7 5 3

Contents

From ghoulies and ghosties,
Long-leggedy beasties,
And things that go BUMP *in the night,*
Good Lord deliver us.

Ghosts Galore

Ghosts gather at close of day,
Haunting houses so they say,
Owls hooting, eerie cries,
Silent voices, silent eyes.
This is the night of the ghosts' high noon,
Shades of the dead shadow the moon.

Ghostly figures weave to and fro,
A groaning sound, an eerie glow,
Listen—the wind whispers in the trees,
Oo—oo—ah—ah! moans the breeze.
Riddle me riddle, who knocks there?
Enter slowly—if you dare!

ROBERT FISHER

The Man Who Wasn't There

Yesterday upon the stair
I met the man who wasn't there;
He wasn't there again today,
I wish, I wish, he'd go away.

I've seen his shapeless shadow-coat
Beneath the stairway, hanging about;
And outside, muffled in a cloak
The same colour as the dark;

I've seen him in a black, black suit
Shaking, under the broken light;
I've seen him swim across the floor
And disappear beneath the door;

And once, I almost heard his breath
Behind me, running up the path:
Inside, he leant against the wall,
And turned . . . and was no one at all.

Yesterday upon the stair,
I met the man who wasn't there;
He wasn't there again today,
I wish, I wish, he'd go away.

BRIAN LEE

Green Man in the Garden

Green man in the garden
  Staring from the tree,
Why do you look so long and hard
  Through the pane at me?

Your eyes are dark as holly,
  Of sycamore your horns,
Your bones are made of elder-branch,
  Your teeth are made of thorns.

Your hat is made of ivy-leaf,
  Of bark your dancing shoes,
And evergreen and green and green
  Your jacket and shirt and trews.

Leave your house and leave your land
  And throw away the key,
And never look behind, he creaked,
  And come and live with me.

I bolted up the window,
  I bolted up the door,
I drew the blind that I should find
  The green man never more.

But when I softly turned the stair
  As I went up to bed,
I saw the green man standing there.
  Sleep well, my friend, he said.

CHARLES CAUSLEY

Who's That?

Who's that
stopping at
my door in the
dark, deep
in the dead of the moonless night?

Who's
that in the quiet
blackness,
darker than dark?

Who
turns the han-
dle of my door, who
turns the old brass hand-
le of
my door with never a sound, the handle
that always
creaks and rattles and
squeaks but
now
turns
without a sound, slowly
slowly
          slowly
                    round?

Who's that moving through the floor
as if it were a lake, an open door? Who
is it who passes through
what can never be passed through,
who passes through
the rocking-chair
without rocking it,
who passes through
the table without knocking it, who
walks out of the cupboard without unlocking it?
Who's that? Who plays with my toys
with no noise, no
noise?

Who's that? Who is it
silent and silver
as things in mirrors, who's
as slow as feathers,
shy as the shivers,
light as a fly?

Who's that who's that
as close as
close as a hug, a kiss—

Who's THIS?

JAMES KIRKUP

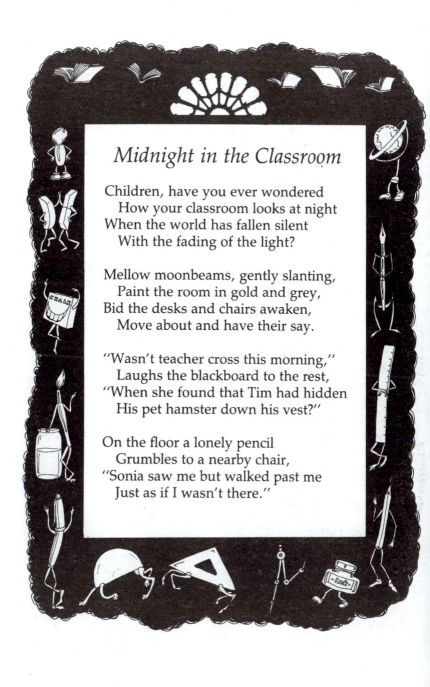

Midnight in the Classroom

Children, have you ever wondered
  How your classroom looks at night
When the world has fallen silent
  With the fading of the light?

Mellow moonbeams, gently slanting,
  Paint the room in gold and grey,
Bid the desks and chairs awaken,
  Move about and have their say.

"Wasn't teacher cross this morning,"
  Laughs the blackboard to the rest,
"When she found that Tim had hidden
  His pet hamster down his vest?"

On the floor a lonely pencil
  Grumbles to a nearby chair,
"Sonia saw me but walked past me
  Just as if I wasn't there."

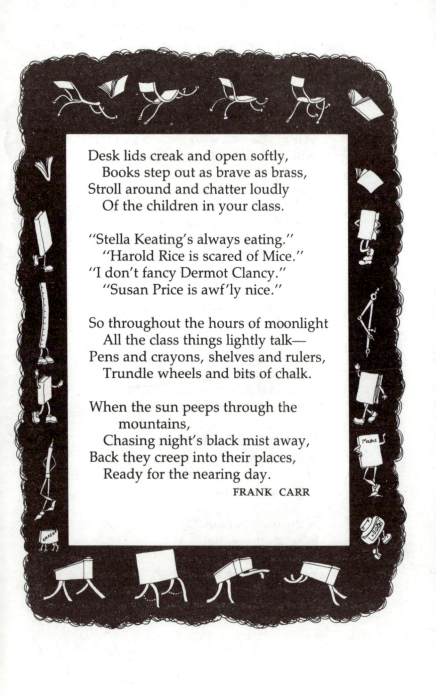

Desk lids creak and open softly,
  Books step out as brave as brass,
Stroll around and chatter loudly
  Of the children in your class.

"Stella Keating's always eating."
  "Harold Rice is scared of Mice."
"I don't fancy Dermot Clancy."
  "Susan Price is awf'ly nice."

So throughout the hours of moonlight
  All the class things lightly talk—
Pens and crayons, shelves and rulers,
  Trundle wheels and bits of chalk.

When the sun peeps through the
    mountains,
  Chasing night's black mist away,
Back they creep into their places,
  Ready for the nearing day.

FRANK CARR

The Secret Brother

Jack lived in the green-house
When I was six,
With glass and with tomato plants,
Not with slates and bricks.

I didn't have a brother,
Jack became mine.
Nobody could see him,
He never gave a sign.

Just beyond the rockery,
By the apple-tree,
Jack and his old mother lived,
Only for me.

With a tin telephone
Held beneath the sheet,
I would talk to Jack each night.
We would never meet.

Once my sister caught me,
Said, "He isn't there.
Down among the flower-pots
Cramm the gardener

Is the only person."
I said nothing, but
Let her go on talking.
Yet I moved Jack out.

He and his old mother
Did a midnight flit.
No one knew his number:
I had altered it.

Only I could see
The sagging washing-line
And my brother making
Our own secret sign.

ELIZABETH JENNINGS

Nasty Night

Whose are the hands you hear
Pulling the roof apart?
What stamps its hoof
Between the bedroom ceiling and the slates?

ROY FULLER

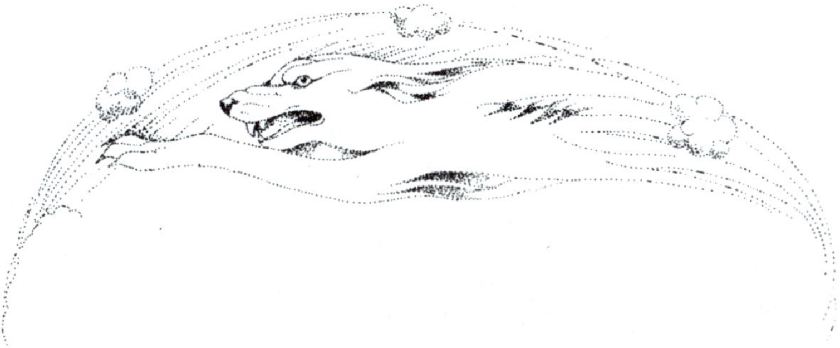

The Riddle

"What is it that goes round and round the house"
The riddle began. A wolf, we thought, or a ghost?
Our cold backs turned to the chink in the kitchen shutter,

The range made our small scared faces warm as toast.

But now the cook is dead and the cooking, no doubt, electric,
No room for draught or dream, for child or mouse,
Though we, in another place, still put ourselves the question:
What *is* it that goes round and round the house?

LOUIS MACNEICE

A Boy's Friend

I have a secret friend
With whom I never quarrel.
I'm Watson to his Holmes,
He's Hardy to my Laurel.

I'm greedy for his calls
And leave him with sad heart.
He thinks of marvellous games.
He mends what comes apart.

Though when he isn't here
I can't recall his face,
I'm always glancing at
That slightly freckled space.

His name's quite ordinary
But seems unusual.
His brain's stocked like a shop.
His talk is comical.

Often with other friends
Play ends in biffs and screams:
With him, play calmly goes
Through dusk—and even dreams.

ROY FULLER

The Handkerchief Ghost

There is a ghost
That eats handkerchiefs;
It keeps you company
On all your travels, and
Eats your handkerchiefs
Out of your trunk, your
Bed, your washstand,
Like a bird eating
Out of your hand—not
All of them and not
All at one go. With
Eighteen handkerchiefs
You set out, a proud mariner,
On the Seas of the Unknown;
With eight or perhaps
Seven you come back, the
Despair of the housewife.

CHRISTIAN MORGENSTERN
(Translated by W. D. Snodgrass)

Skilly Oogan

Skilly Oogan's no one you can see,
And no one else can be his friend but me,
Skilly lives where swallows live, away up high
Beneath the topmost eaves against the sky.
When all the world's asleep on moonlit nights
Up on our roof he flies his cobweb kites.
He has an acorn boat that, when it rains,
He sails in gutters, even down the drains.
Sometimes he hides in letters that I write—
Snug in the envelope and out of sight,
On six-cent stamps he travels in all weathers
And with the midnight owl returns on silent feathers.
In summer time he rides the dragonflies
Above the pond, and looks in bullfrogs' eyes
For his reflection when he combs his hair.
And sometimes when I want him he's not there;
But mostly Skilly Oogan's where I think he'll be,
And no one even knows his name but me.

RUSSELL HOBAN

Queer Things

"Very, very queer things have been happening to me
  In some of the places where I've been.
I went to the pillar-box this morning with a letter
  And a hand came out and took it in.

"When I got home again, I thought I'd have
  A glass of spirits to steady myself;
And I take my bible oath, but that bottle and glass
  Came a-hopping down off the shelf.

"No, no, I says, I'd better take no spirits,
  And I sat down to have a cup of tea;
And blowed if my old pair of carpet-slippers
  Didn't walk across the carpet to me!

"So I took my newspaper and went into the park,
  And looked round to see no one was near,
When a voice right out of the middle of the paper
  Started reading the news bold and clear!

"Well, I guess there's some magician out to help me,
  So perhaps there's no need for alarm;
And if I manage not to anger him,
  Why should he do me any harm?"

JAMES REEVES

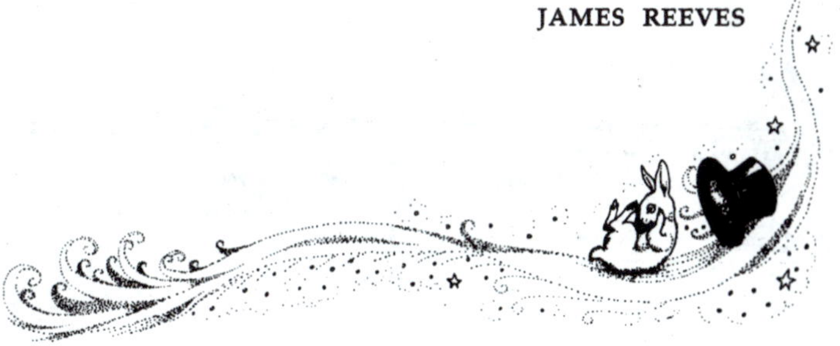

The Silent Eye

On the moon lives an eye.
It flies about in the sky,
Staring, glaring, or just peering.
You can't see what it uses for steering.
It is about the size of a large owl,
But has no feathers, and so is by no means a fowl.
Sometimes it zips overhead from horizon to horizon
Then you know it has been something surprisin'.
Mostly it hovers just above you and stares
Rudely down into your most private affairs.
Nobody minds it much, they say it has charm.
It has no mouth or hands, so how could it do harm?
Besides, as I say, it has these appealing ways.
When you are sitting sadly under crushing dismays,
This eye floats up and gazes at you like a mourner,
Then droops and wilts and a huge tear sags from its corner,
And soon it is sobbing and expressing such woe
You begin to wish it would stop it and just go.

TED HUGHES

The Silent Voices

When the dumb hour, clothed in black,
Brings the dreams about my bed,
Call me not so often back,
Silent voices of the dead,
Toward the lowland ways behind me,
And the sunlight that is gone!
Call me rather, silent voices,
Forward to the starry track
Glimmering up the heights beyond me,
On, and always on!

ALFRED, LORD TENNYSON

The Dark Wood

In the dark, dark wood, there was
  a dark, dark house,
And in that dark, dark house, there was
  a dark, dark room,
And in that dark, dark room, there was
  a dark, dark cupboard,
And in that dark, dark cupboard, there was
  a dark, dark shelf,
And on that dark, dark shelf, there was
  a dark, dark box,
And in that dark, dark box, there was a
  GHOST!

ANON

Mr Nobody

I know a funny little man,
As quiet as a mouse.
He does the mischief that is done
In everybody's house.
Though no one ever sees his face,
Yet one and all agree
That every plate we break, was cracked
By Mr Nobody.

'Tis he who always tears our books,
Who leaves the door ajar.
He picks the buttons from our shirts,
And scatters pins afar.
That squeaking door will always squeak
For prithee, don't you see?
We leave the oiling to be done
By Mr Nobody.

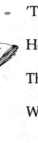

He puts the damp wood upon the fire,
That kettles will not boil:
His are the feet that bring in mud
And all the carpets soil.
The papers that so oft are lost—
Who had them last but he?
There's no one tosses them about
But Mr Nobody.

ANON

HOME
SWEET
HOME

The Hairy Toe

Once there was a woman went out to pick beans,
and she found a Hairy Toe.
She took the Hairy Toe home with her,
and that night, when she went to bed,
the wind began to moan and groan.
Away off in the distance
she seemed to hear a voice crying,
"Where's my Hair-r-ry To-o-oe?
Who's got my Hair-r-ry To-o-oe?"

The woman scrooched down,
'way down under the covers,
and about that time
the wind appeared to hit the house,

smoosh,

and the old house creaked and cracked
like something was trying to get in.
The voice had come nearer,
almost at the door now,
and it said,
"Where's my Hair-r-ry To-o-oe?
Who's got my Hair-r-ry To-o-oe?"

The woman scrooched further down
under the covers
and pulled them tight around her head.

With Her Head Tucked Underneath Her Arm

In the Tower of London, large as life
The ghost of Ann Boleyn walks, they declare.
Poor Ann Boleyn was once King Henry's wife—
Until he made the Headsman bob her hair!
Ah yes! he did her wrong long years ago
And she comes up at night to tell him so.

With her head tucked underneath her arm
She walks the Bloody Tower!
With her head tucked underneath her arm
At the Midnight hour.
Along the draughty corridors for miles and miles she goes,
She often catches cold, poor thing, it's cold there when it blows,
And it's awfully awkward for the Queen to have to blow her nose
With her head tucked underneath her arm!

Sometimes gay King Henry gives a spread
For all his pals and gals—a ghostly crew.
The headsman carves the joint and cuts the bread,
Then in comes Ann Boleyn to "queer" the "do",
She holds her head up with a wild war whoop,
And Henry cries "Don't drop it in the soup!"

With her head tucked underneath her arm
She walks the Bloody Tower!
With her head tucked underneath her arm
At the Midnight hour!

R. P. WESTON and BERT LEE

Voices

I heard those voices today again:
Voices of women and children, down in that hollow
Of blazing light into which swoops the tree-darkened lane
Before it mounts up into the shadow again.

I turned the bend—just as always before
There was no one at all down there in the sunlit hollow;
Only ferns in the wall, foxgloves by the hanging door
Of that blind old desolate cottage. And just as before

I noticed the leaping glitter of light
Where the stream runs under the lane; in that mine-dark
  archway
—Water and stones unseen as though in the gloom of
  night—
Like glittering fish slithers and leaps the light.

I waited long at the bend of the lane,
But heard only the murmuring water under the archway.
Yet I tell you, I've been to that place again and again,
And always, in summer weather, those voices are plain,
Down near that broken house, just where the tree-darkened
  lane
Swoops into the hollow of light before mounting to shadow
  again.

FRANCES BELLERBY

Prince Kano

In a dark wood Prince Kano lost his way
And searched in vain through the long summer's day.
At last, when night was near, he came in sight
Of a small clearing filled with yellow light,
And there, bending beside his brazier, stood
A charcoal burner wearing a black hood.
The Prince cried out for joy: "Good friend, I'll give
What you will ask: guide me to where I live."
The man pulled back his hood: he had no face—
Where it should be there was an empty space.

Half dead with fear the Prince staggered away,
Rushed blindly through the wood till break of day;
And then he saw a larger clearing, filled
With houses, people; but his soul was chilled,
He looked around for comfort, and his search
Led him inside a small, half-empty church
Where monks prayed. "Father," to one he said,
"I've seen a dreadful thing; I am afraid."
"What did you see, my son?" "I saw a man
Whose face was like . . ." and, as the Prince began,
The monk drew back his hood and seemed to hiss,
Pointing to where his face should be, "Like this?"

EDWARD LOWBURY

The Voice in the Tunnel

The end of the tunnel was dark
I was alone
Or thought I was
So to cheer myself up I called
"Anyone there?"
Then came the voice
  There   there

I tried again
"Hello!"
  hello
"Are you near?"
  Near   near
"WHO are you?"
  Who   whooooo?

I got out of that tunnel pretty quick
And with each step I heard another
strange and distant

Now far away
I cannot hear that voice
But still I wonder what it is saying
in the dark
  at the end of the tunnel.

ROBERT FISHER

Oo-oo-ah-ah!

A woman in a churchyard sat,
  Oo-oo-ah-ah!
Very short and very fat,
  Oo-oo-ah-ah!
She saw three corpses carried in,
  Oo-oo-ah-ah!
Very tall and very thin,
  Oo-oo-ah-ah!

Woman to the corpses said,
  Oo-oo-ah-ah!
"Shall I be like you when I am dead?"
  Oo-oo-ah-ah!

Corpses to the woman said,
  Oo-oo-ah-ah!
"Yes, you'll be like us when you are dead,"
  Oo-oo-ah-ah!
Woman to the corpses said—

  (Silence)

ANON

The Magic Wood

The wood is full of shining eyes,
The wood is full of creeping feet,
The wood is full of tiny cries:
You must not go to the wood at night!

I met a man with eyes of glass
And a finger as curled as the wriggling worm,
And hair all red with rotting leaves,
And a stick that hissed like a summer snake.

The wood is full of shining eyes,
The wood is full of creeping feet,
The wood is full of tiny cries:
You must not go to the wood at night!

He sang me a song in backwards words,
And drew me a dragon in the air.
I saw his teeth through the back of his head,
And a rat's eyes winking from his hair.

The wood is full of shining eyes,
The wood is full of creeping feet,
The wood is full of tiny cries:
You must not go to the wood at night!

He made me a penny out of a stone,
And showed me the way to catch a lark
With a straw and a nut and a whispered word
And a penn'orth of ginger wrapped up in a leaf.

The wood is full of shining eyes,
The wood is full of creeping feet,
The wood is full of tiny cries:
You must not go to the wood at night!

He asked me my name, and where I lived;
I told him a name from my Book of Tales;
He asked me to come with him into the wood
And dance with the Kings from under the hills.

The wood is full of shining eyes,
The wood is full of creeping feet,
The wood is full of tiny cries:
You must not go to the wood at night!

But I saw that his eyes were turning to fire;
I watched the nails grow on his wriggling hand;
And I said my prayers, all out in a rush,
And found myself safe on my father's land.

Oh, the wood is full of shining eyes,
The wood is full of creeping feet,
The wood is full of tiny cries:
You must not go to the wood at night!

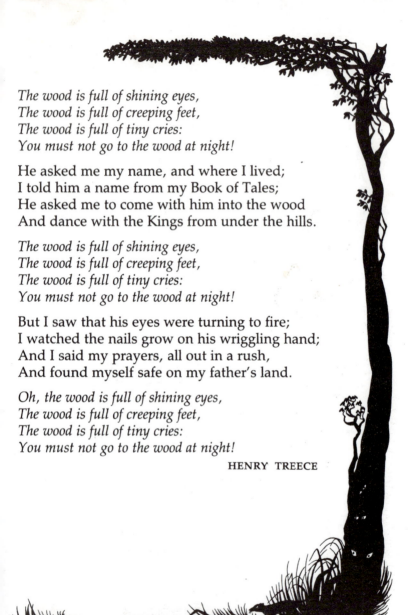

HENRY TREECE

The Visitor

A crumbling churchyard, the sea and the moon;
The waves had gouged out grave and bone;
A man was walking, late and alone . . .

He saw a skeleton white on the ground,
A ring on a bony hand he found.

He ran home to his wife and gave her the ring.
"Oh, where did you get it?" He said not a thing.

"It's the prettiest ring in the world," she said,
As it glowed on her finger. They skipped off to bed.

At midnight they woke. In the dark outside,
"Give me my ring!" a chill voice cried.

"What was that, William? What did it say?"
"Don't worry, my dear. It'll soon go away."

"I'm coming!" A skeleton opened the door.
"Give me my ring!" It was crossing the floor.

"What was that, William? What did it say?"
"Don't worry, my dear. It'll soon go away."

"I'm touching you now! I'm climbing the bed."
The wife pulled the sheet right over her head.

It was torn from her grasp and tossed in the air:
"I'll drag you out of the bed by the hair!"

"What was that, William? What did it say?"
"Throw the ring through the window! THROW IT AWAY!"

She threw it. The skeleton leapt from the sill,
Scooped up the ring and clattered downhill,
Fainter . . . and fainter . . . Then all was still.

IAN SERRAILLIER

The Ghost and the Skeleton

A skeleton once in Khartoum
Invited a ghost to his room.
They spent the whole night
In the eeriest fight
As to who should be frightened of whom.

ANON

The Glimpse

She sped through the door
And, following in haste,
And stirred to the core,
I entered hot-faced;
But I could not find her,
No sign was behind her.
"Where is she?" I said:
—"Who?" they asked that sat there;
"Not a soul's come in sight."
—"A maid with red hair."
—"Ah." They paled. "She is dead.
People see her at night,
But you are the first
On whom she has burst
In the keen common light."

It was ages ago,
When I was quite strong:
I have waited since,—O,
I have waited so long!
—Yea, I set me to own
The house, where now lone
I dwell in void rooms
Booming hollow as tombs!
But I never come near her,
Though nightly I hear her.
And my cheek has grown thin
And my hair has grown gray
With this waiting therein;
But she still keeps away!

THOMAS HARDY

Johnny Dow

Who lies here?
I, Johnny Dow.
Who! Johnny is that you?
Aye, man, but I'm dead now.

ANON

Song of Two Ghosts

My friend
This is a wide world
We're travelling over
Walking on the moonlight.

ANON

(Indian Song from Omaha, North America)

A Meeting

When George began to climb all unawares
He saw a horrible face at the top of the stairs.

The rats came tumbling down the planks,
Pushing past without a word of thanks.

The rats were thin, the stairs were tall,
But the face at the top was the worst of all.

It wasn't the ghost of his father or mother.
When they are laid there's always another.

It wasn't the ghost of people he knew.
It was worse than this, shall I tell you who?

It was himself, oh what a disgrace.
And soon they were standing face to face.

At first they pretended neither cared
But when they met they stood and stared.

One started to smile and the other to frown,
And one moved up and the other moved down.

But which emerged and which one stays,
Nobody will know till the end of his days.

GEORGE D. PAINTER

Emperors of the Island

There is the story of a deserted island
where five men walked down to the bay.

The story of the island is
that three men would two men slay:

Three men dug two graves in the sand,
three men stood on the sea-wet rock,
three shadows moved away.

There is the story of a deserted island
where three men walked down to the bay.

The story of this island is
that two men would one man slay.

Two men dug one grave in the sand,
two men stood on the sea-wet rock,
two shadows moved away.

There is the story of a deserted island
where two men walked down to the bay.
The story of this island is
that one man would one man slay.

One man dug one grave in the sand,
one man stood on the sea-wet rock,
one shadow moved away.

There is the story of a deserted island
where four ghosts walked down to the bay.

The story of this island is
that four ghosts would one man slay.

Four ghosts dug one grave in the sand,
four ghosts stood on the sea-wet rock;
five ghosts moved away.

DANNIE ABSE

The Spunky

The Spunky he went like a sad little flame,
All, all alone.
All out on the zogs[1] and a-down the lane,
All, all alone.
A tinker came by that was full of ale,
And into the mud he went head over tail,
All, all alone.

A crotchety farmer came riding by,
All, all alone.
He cursed him low and he cursed him high,
All, all alone.
The Spunky he up and he led him astray,
The pony were foundered until it were day,
All, all alone.

There came an old granny—she see the small ghost,
All, all alone.
"Yew poor liddle soul all a-cold, a-lost,
All, all alone.
I'll give 'ee a criss-cross to save 'ee bide;
Be off to the church and make merry inside,
All, all alone."

The Spunky he laughed, "Here I'll galley[2] no more!"
All, all alone.
And off he did wiver[3] and in at the door,
All, all alone.
The souls they did sing for to end his pain,
There's no little Spunky a-down the lane,
All, all alone.

ANON

[1] fields [2] linger [3] waver

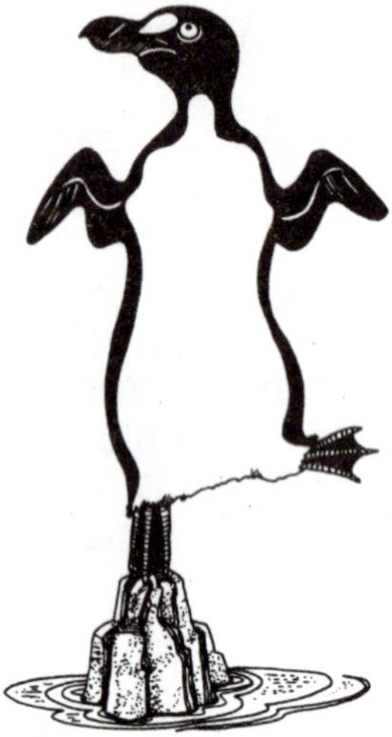

The Great Auk's Ghost

The great auk's ghost rose on one leg,
  Sighed thrice and three times winkt,
And turned and poached a phantom egg,
  And muttered, "I'm extinct."

RALPH HODGSON

Sweet William's Ghost

There came a ghost to Margret's door,
With many a grievous groan,
And then he knocked upon the door,
But answer made she none.

"Is that my father Philip?
Or is it my brother John?
Or is it my true love Willie,
From Scotland now come home?"

"It's not your father Philip,
It's not your brother John,
But it's your true love Willie,
From Scotland now come home."

"O sweet Margret! O dear Margret!
I pray you speak to me;
Give me faith and love, Margret,
As I gave it to thee."

"That faith and love you'll never get,
That prize you'll never win,
Until you come inside my house
And kiss my cheek and chin."

"If I should come within your house,
I am no earthly man;
And should I kiss your rosy lips,
Your days will not be long."

"O sweet Margret, O dear Margret,
I pray you speak to me;
Give me faith and love, Margret,
As I gave it to thee."

"That faith and love you'll never get.
That prize you'll never win,
Until you take me to your church,
And wed me with a ring."

"My bones are buried in that church-yard,
Afar beyond the sea,
And it is but my spirit, Margret,
That's now speaking to thee."

She stretched out her lily-white hand,
And tried to do her best,
"Hey, there's your faith and love, Willy,
God send your soul good rest."

Now she has kilted her robes of green
A piece below the knee,
And all the live-long winter night
The dead corpse followed she.

"Is there any room at your head, Willy?
Or any room at your feet?
Or any room at your side, Willy,
Where in that I may creep?"

"There's no room at my head, Margret,
There's no room at my feet;
There's no room at my side, Margret,
My coffin's made complete."

Then up and crew the red, red cock,
And up and crew the grey;
"It's time, it's time, my dear Margret,
That you were going away."

No more the ghost to Margret said,
But with a grievous groan
It vanished in a cloud of mist,
And left her all alone.

"O stay, my only true-love, stay,"
The constant Margret cried;
Pale grew her cheeks, she closed her eyes,
Stretched her soft limbs, and died.

ANON
(Old Ballad, modernized)

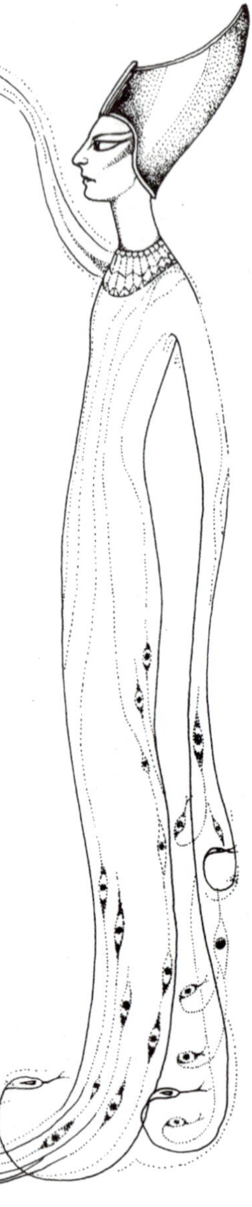

Queen Nefertiti

Spin a coin, spin a coin,
  All fall down;
Queen Nefertiti
  Stalks through the town.

Over the pavements
  Her feet go clack,
Her legs are as tall
  As a chimney stack;

Her fingers flicker
  Like snakes in the air,
The walls split open
  At her green-eyed stare;

Her voice is thin
  As the ghosts of bees;
She will crumble your bones,
  She will make your blood freeze.

Spin a coin, spin a coin,
  All fall down;
Queen Nefertiti
  Stalks through the town.

ANON

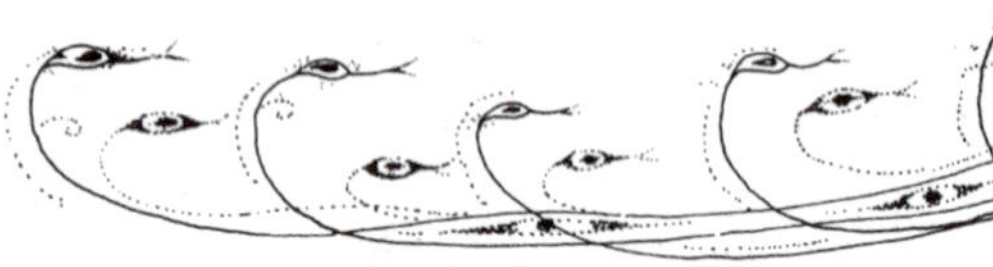

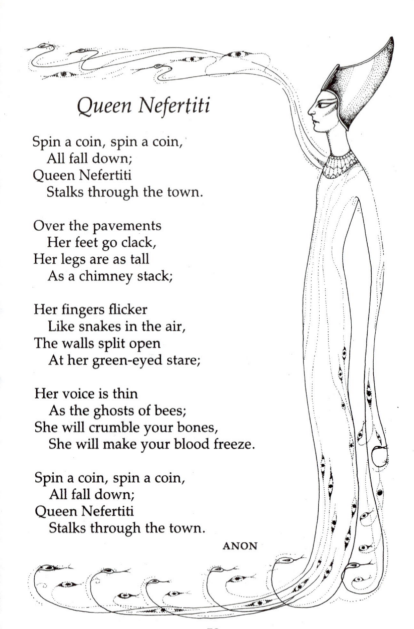

Shadow-Bride

There was a man who dwelt alone,
  as day and night went past.
He sat as still as carven stone,
  and yet no shadow cast.
The white owls perched upon his head
  beneath the winter moon;
they wiped their beaks and thought him dead
  under the stars of June.

There came a lady clad in grey
  in the twilight shining;
one moment she would stand and stay,
  her hair with flowers entwining.
He woke, as had he sprung of stone,
  and broke the spell that bound him;
he clasped her fast, both flesh and bone,
  and wrapped her shadow round him.

There never more she walks her ways
  by sun or moon or star;
she dwells below where neither days
  nor any nights there are.
But once a year when caverns yawn
  and hidden things awake,
they dance together then till dawn
  and a single shadow make.

J. R. R. TOLKIEN

The Old Wife and the Ghost

There was an old wife and she lived all alone
In a cottage not far from Hitchin:
And one bright night, by the full moon light,
Comes a ghost right into her kitchen.

About that kitchen neat and clean
The ghost goes pottering round.
But the poor old wife is deaf as a boot
And so hears never a sound.

The ghost blows up the kitchen fire,
As bold as bold can be;
He helps himself from the larder shelf,
But never a sound hears she.

He blows on his hands to make them warm,
And whistles aloud "Whee-hee!"
But still as a sack the old soul lies
And never a sound hears she.

From corner to corner he runs about,
And into the cupboard he peeps;
He rattles the door and bumps on the floor,
But still the old wife sleeps.

Jangle and bang go the pots and pans,
As he throws them all around;
And the plates and mugs and dishes and jugs,
He flings them all to the ground.

Madly the ghost tears up and down
And screams like a storm at sea;
And at last the old wife stirs in her bed—
And it's "Drat those mice," says she.

Then the first cock crows and morning shows
And the troublesome ghost's away.
But oh! what a pickle the poor wife sees
When she gets up next day.

"Them's tidy big mice," the old wife thinks,
And off she goes to Hitchin,
And a tidy big cat she fetches back
To keep the mice from her kitchen.

JAMES REEVES

The Ghosts' High Noon

When the night wind howls in the chimney cowls, and the bat in the moonlight flies,
And inky clouds, like funeral shrouds, sail over the midnight skies—
When the footpads quail at the night-bird's wail, and black dogs bay the moon,
Then is the spectres' holiday—then is the ghosts' high noon!

As the sob of the breeze sweeps over the trees, and the mists lie low on the fen,
From grey tombstones are gathered the bones that once were women and men,
And away they go, with a mop and a mow, to the revel that ends too soon,
For cockcrow limits our holiday—the dead of the night's high noon!

And then each ghost with his ladye-toast to their churchyard beds take flight,
With a kiss, perhaps, on her lantern chaps, and a grisly grim "good night";
Till the welcome knell of the midnight bell rings forth its jolliest tune,
And ushers our next high holiday—the dead of the night's high noon!

W. S. GILBERT

The Term

A rumpled sheet
of brown paper
about the length

and apparent bulk
of a man was
rolling with the

wind slowly over
and over in
the street as

a car drove down
upon it and
crushed it to

the ground. Unlike
a man it rose
again rolling

with the wind over
and over to be as
it was before.

WILLIAM CARLOS WILLIAMS

Kingdom of Mist

I ride through a kingdom of mist
where farms drown in a phantom sea
and May piles up in the hedge like snow
waiting to melt in tomorrow's sun.

Young wheat lies down where May-winds blew
and larks are earthbound by the stars.
A heron glides between the trees
that hold the river to its course.

Here pebbles slowly turn to snails
and spiders' webs are spun with glass.
Small shells fly off as frightened moths
and cows become as druid stones.

Only the mist moves as a ghost
loving the land with limbs of fur
and whispered words grow grey as breath
rising into the frosting air.

And night comes down where day once grew,
lights ripple through this thin white sea,
while in the village children sleep
never to know they slept in sky.

EDWARD STOREY

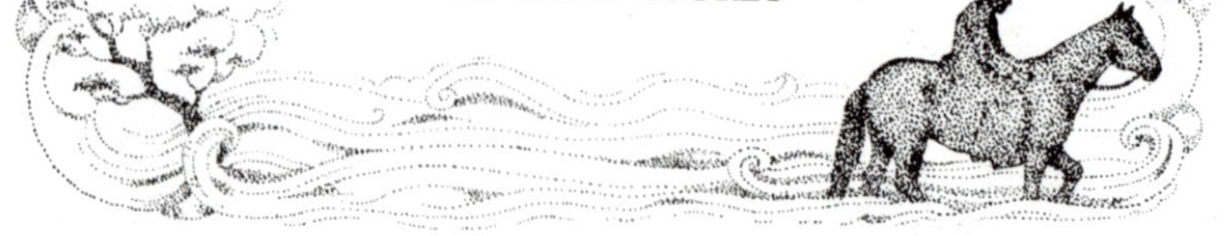

Ghosts

I to a crumpled cabin came
Upon a hillside high,
And with me was a withered dame
As weariful as I.
"It used to be our home," said she;
"How I remember well!
Oh that our happy hearth should be
Today an empty shell!"

The door was flailing in the storm
That deafed us with its din;
The roof that kept us once so warm
Now let the snow-drift in.
The floor sagged to the sod below,
The walls caved crazily;
We only heard the wind of woe
Where once was glow and glee.

So there we stood disconsolate
Beneath the Midnight Dome,
An ancient miner and his mate,
Before our wedded home,
Where we had known such love and cheer . . .
I sighed, then soft she said:
"Do not regret—remember, dear,
We, too, are dead."

ROBERT SERVICE

There Were Three Ghostesses

There were three ghostesses
Sitting on postesses
Eating buttered toastesses
And greasing their fistesses
Right up to their wristesses.
Weren't they beastesses
To make such feastesses!

ANON

The Ghost

"Who knocks?" "I, who was beautiful,
  Beyond all dreams to restore,
I, from the roots of the dark thorn am hither.
  And knock on the door."

"Who speaks?" "I—once was my speech
  Sweet as the bird's on the air,
When echo lurks by the waters to heed;
  'Tis I speak thee fair."

"Dark is the hour!" "Ay, and cold."
  "Lone is my house." "Ah, but mine?"
"Sight, touch, lips, eyes yearned in vain."
  "Long dead these to thine. . . ."

Silence. Still faint on the porch
  Brake the flames of the stars.
In gloom groped a hope-wearied hand
  Over keys, bolts, and bars.

A face peered. All the grey night
  In chaos of vacancy shone;
Nought but vast sorrow was there—
  The sweet cheat gone.

WALTER DE LA MARE

Green Candles

"There's someone at the door," said gold candlestick:
"Let her in quick, let her in quick!"
"There is a small hand groping at the handle.
Why don't you turn it?" asked green candle.

"Don't go, don't go," said the Hepplewhite chair,
"Lest you find a strange lady there."
"Yes, stay where you are," whispered the white wall:
"There is nobody there at all."

"I know her little foot," grey carpet said:
"Who but I should know her light tread?"
"She shall come in," answered the open door,
"And not," said the room, "go out any more."

HUMBERT WOLFE

At Home

When I was dead, my spirit turned
  To seek the much-frequented house:
I passed the door, and saw my friends
  Feasting beneath the green orange boughs;
From hand to hand they pushed the wine,
  They sucked the pulp of plum and peach;
They sang, they jested, and they laughed,
  For each was loved of each.

I listened to their honest chat:
  Said one: "To-morrow we shall be
Plod plod along the featureless sands
  And coasting miles and miles of sea."
Said one: "Before the turn of tide
  We will achieve the eyrie-seat."
Said one: "To-morrow shall be like
  To-day, but much more sweet."

"To-morrow," said they, strong with hope,
  And dwelt upon the pleasant way:
"To-morrow," cried they one and all,
  While no one spoke of yesterday.
Their life stood full at blessed noon;
  I, only I, had passed away:
"To-morrow and to-day," they cried;
  I was of yesterday.

I shivered comfortless, but cast
  No chill across the tablecloth;
I all-forgotten shivered, sad
  To stay and yet to part how loth:
I passed from the familiar room,
  I who from love had passed away,
Like the remembrance of a guest
  That tarrieth but a day.

CHRISTINA ROSSETTI

I Once Dressed Up

I once dressed up as a ghost
It was wet and I was bored
Waiting for Mum to come home
Drawing pictures on the windows
And chewing a bit of cheese
Then it hit me—this idea
So I got an old sheet from the airing cupboard
I was only six at the time or seven
And put it over my head
Couldn't see couldn't hear anything
Except the sound of breathing
The world went white then black
I waited
A lonely ghost by the stairs
Then I heard a bang and the sound
   of f–o–o–t–s–t–e–p–s
      coming closer
"*Hellooooo*" said a creepy voice
I shot out from that sheet double quick
The sheet was white and so was I
"It's only me," I said
Mum laughed
It can be quite scary being a ghost

ROBERT FISHER

Teeny Tiny Ghost

A teeny tiny ghost
no bigger than a mouse,
at most,
lived in a great big house.

It's hard to haunt
a great big house
when you're a teeny tiny ghost
no bigger than a mouse,
at most.

He did what he could do.

So every dark and stormy night—
the kind that shakes a house with fright—
if you stood still and listened right,
you'd hear a
teeny
tiny
BOO!

LILIAN MOORE

The Empty House

Where the lone wind on the hilltop
Shakes the thistles as it passes,
Stirs the quiet-ticking grasses
That keep time outside the door,
Stands a house that's grey and silent;
No one lives there any more.

Wending through the broken windows,
Every season and its weather
Whisper in those rooms together:
Summer's warm and wandering rains
Rot the leaves of last year's autumn,
Warp the floors that winter stains.

In a papered hall a clock-shape,
Dim and pale on yellowed flowers,
Still remains where rang the hours
Of a clock that's lost and gone.
And the fading ghost keeps no-time
On the wall it lived upon.

On a stairway where no footsteps
Stir the dusty sunlight burning
Sit the patient shadows turning
Speechless faces to the wall
While they hear the silent striking
Of that no-clock in the hall.

"Dawn of no-time! Noon of no-time!"
Cries the phantom echo chiming,
And the shadows, moving, miming,
Slowly shift before the light.
But no eye has seen their motion
When the clock says, "No-time night!"

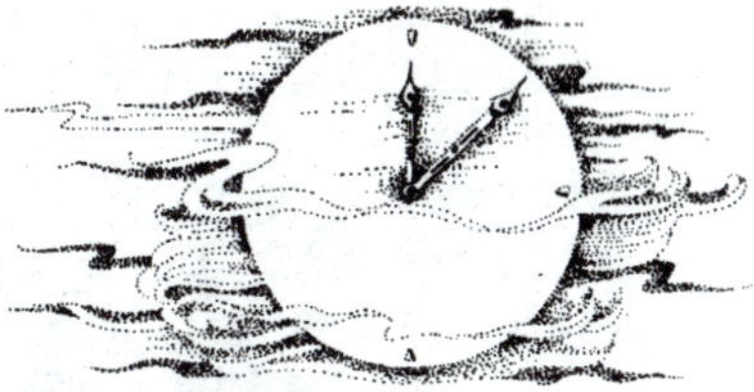

No eye has seen them dancing
In their blackness fell and bright,
To a silent tune
In the dark of the moon
When the clock sings no-time night.

RUSSELL HOBAN

Haunted

Black hill
black hall
all still
owl's grey cry
edges shrill
castle night.

Woken eye
round in fright;
what lurks walks
in castle rustle?

Hand cold
held hand
the moving roving
urging thing;
dreamed margin

voiceless
noiseless
HEARD
feared
a ghost passed

black hill
black hall
all still
owl's grey cry
edges shrill
castle night.

WILLIAM MAYNE

The Ghost in the Garden

For clanking and lank
The Armoured Knight
Rides down the dank
Shadows in flight;
Grass stiff with frost
Shows grey as steel
As the Conquering Ghost
Clanks down the hill.
  Now the first cock crows,
  Impudent, frightened, through the dark;
  Then a cold wind blows,
  And that whining dog, Dawn, begins to bark.
Then the Knight in Armour
Passes away,
As the growing clamour
Proclaims, "It is Day."
The trees grow taller,
The gate is shut,
The Knight grows smaller,
                    Goes smaller,
                              And out.

OSBERT SITWELL

Colonel Fazackerley

Colonel Fazackerley Butterworth-Toast
Bought an old castle complete with a ghost,
But someone or other forgot to declare
To Colonel Fazack that the spectre was there.

On the very first evening, while waiting to dine,
The Colonel was taking a fine sherry wine,
When the ghost with a furious flash and a flare,
Shot out of the chimney and shivered, "Beware!"

Colonel Fazackerley put down his glass
And said, "My dear fellow, that's really first class!
I just can't conceive how you do it at all,
I imagine you're going to a Fancy Dress Ball?"

At this, the dread ghost gave a withering cry.
Said the Colonel (his monocle firm in his eye),
"Now just how you do it I wish I could think.
Do sit down and tell me, and please have a drink."

The ghost in his phosphorous cloak gave a roar
And floated about between ceiling and floor.
He walked through a wall and returned through a pane
And backed up the chimney and came down again.

Said the Colonel, "With laughter I'm feeling quite weak!"
(As trickles of merriment ran down his cheek).
"My house-warming party I hope you won't spurn.
You must say you'll come and you'll give us a turn!"

At this the poor spectre—quite out of his wits—
Proceeded to shake himself almost to bits.
He rattled his chains and he clattered his bones
And he filled the whole castle with mumbles and moans.

But Colonel Fazackerley, just as before,
Was simply delighted and called out, "Encore!"
At which the ghost vanished, his efforts in vain,
And never was seen at the castle again.

"Oh dear, what a pity!" said Colonel Fazack.
"I don't know his name, so I can't call him back."
And then with a smile that was hard to define,
Colonel Fazackerley went in to dine.

CHARLES CAUSLEY

Two's Company

The sad story of the man who didn't believe in ghosts

They said the house was haunted, but
He laughed at them and said, "Tut, tut!
I've never heard such tittle-tattle
As ghosts that groan and chains that rattle;
And just to prove I'm in the right,
Please leave me here to spend the night."

They winked absurdly, tried to smother
Their ignorant laughter, nudged each other,
And left him just as dusk was falling
With a hunchback moon and screech-owls calling.
Not that this troubled him one bit;
In fact, he was quite glad of it,
Knowing it's every sane man's mission
To contradict all superstition.

But what is that? Outside it seemed
As if chains rattled, someone screamed!
Come, come, it's merely nerves, he's certain
(But just the same, he draws the curtain).
The stroke of twelve—but there's no clock!
He shuts the door and turns the lock
(Of course, he knows that no one's there,
But no harm's done by taking care!)
Someone's outside—the silly joker,
(He may as well pick up the poker!)
That noise again! He checks the doors,
Shutters the windows, makes a pause

To seek the safest place to hide—
(The cupboard's strong—he creeps inside).
"Not that there's anything to fear,"
He tells himself, when at his ear
A voice breathes softly, "How do you do!
I am the ghost. Pray, who are you?"

RAYMOND WILSON

The Longest Journey in the World

"Last one into bed
has to switch out the light."
It's just the same every night.
There's a race.
I'm ripping off my trousers and shirt,
he's kicking off his shoes and socks.

"My sleeve's stuck."
"This button's too big for its button-hole."
"Have you hidden my pyjamas?"
"Keep your hands off mine."

If you win
you get where it's safe
before the darkness comes—
but if you lose
if you're last
you know what you've got coming up is
the journey from the light switch to your bed
It's the Longest Journey in the World.

"You're last tonight," my brother says.
And he's right.

There is nowhere so dark
as that room in the moment
after I've switched out the light.

There is nowhere so full of dangerous things,
things that love dark places,
things that breathe only when you breathe
and hold their breath when I hold mine.

So I have to say:
"I'm not scared."
That face, grinning in the pattern on the wall,
isn't a face—
"I'm not scared."
That prickle on the back of my neck
is only the label on my pyjama jacket—
"I'm not scared."
That moaning-moaning is nothing
but water in a pipe—
"I'm not scared."

Everything's going to be just fine
as soon as I get into that bed of mine.
Such a terrible shame
it's always the same
it takes so long
it takes so long
it takes so long
to get there.

From the light switch
to my bed
it's the Longest Journey in the World.

MICHAEL ROSEN

Uncle Fred

"There's no such things as ghosts"—
That's what my uncle Fred said
"There's no such things as ghosts
no ghastly ghouls
or ghostly spooks
no wizened witches
nor weird werewolfs
and those that are buried stay buried,"
said my uncle Fred
"and things that go bump in the night
have fallen off the mantelpiece because the cat
knocked them over
all those pale apparitions
are just superstitions
There's no such things as ghosts."

But then Fred died
Poor Uncle Fred
Dead
He died with a smile on his face
I went to his funeral to say goodbye
And when that night I climbed into bed
I heard a small voice
quite close to my head
"There's no such things as ghosts"
was all that it said.

ROBERT FISHER

Old Dan

At night when everyone's asleep
The windows are open and the doors CREAK
But there stands the shadow of an old man
Who walks round the house—
I call him Dan.
No one knows who he is supposed to be
For no one has a chance to see him
But me.

FARAH, aged 11

Acknowledgements

The editor is grateful for permission to use the following copyright material:

"The Man who Wasn't There" from *Late Home* by Brian Lee (Kestrel Books 1976) pp. 29–30 Copyright © 1976 by Brian Lee. Reprinted by permission of Penguin Books Ltd.
"Green Man in the Garden" from *Collected Poems* and "Colonel Fazackerley" from *Figgie Hobbin* by Charles Causley, published by Macmillan, London and Basingstoke.
"Who's That" by James Kirkup.
"Midnight in the Classroom" by Frank Carr. Reprinted by permission of W. Foulsham & Co. Ltd.
"The Secret Brother" from *The Secret Brother* by Elizabeth Jennings, published by Macmillan, London and Basingstoke.
"Nasty Night" from *Poor Roy* (1977) and "A Boy's Friend" from *Seen Grandpa Lately?* (1972) by Roy Fuller, published by André Deutsch Ltd.
"The Riddle" by Louis MacNeice. Reprinted by permission of Faber and Faber Ltd from *The Collected Poems of Louis MacNeice*.
"The Handkerchief Ghost" by Christian Morgenstern, by permission of W. D. Snodgrass.
"Skilly Oogan" and "The Empty House" from *The Pedalling Man* by Russell Hoban, published by World's Work.
"Queer Things" from *The Wandering Moon* by James Reeves, published by William Heinemann Ltd.
"The Silent Eye" by Ted Hughes. Reprinted by permission of Faber and Faber Ltd from *The Earth Owl and Other Moon People* by Ted Hughes.
"Voices" from *Selected Poems* by Frances Bellerby, published by Enitharmon Press.
"Prince Kano" from *Green Magic* by Edward Lowbury, by permission of the author.

"The Magic Wood" by Henry Treece. Copyright © Henry Treece 1945.
"The Visitor" by Ian Serraillier. Copyright © 1980 Ian Serraillier. First published in *A Second Poetry Book* compiled by John Foster (Oxford University Press, 1980).
"A Meeting" by George Painter from *Hist Whist* edited by Dennis Saunders, published by Evans Brothers Ltd.
"Emperors of the Island" from *Tenants of the House* by Dannie Abse, published by Hutchinson Books Ltd. Copyright © 1977 by Dannie Abse.
"The Great Auk's Ghost" from *Collected Poems* by Ralph Hodgson, reprinted by permission of Mrs Hodgson and Macmillan, London and Basingstoke.
"Shadow Bride" from *Adventures of Tom Bombadil* by J. R. R. Tolkien, published by George Allen & Unwin (Publishers) Ltd.
"The Old Wife and the Ghost" from *The Blackbird in the Lilac* by James Reeves (1952). Reprinted by permission of Oxford University Press.
"The Term" by William Carlos Williams, *Collected Earlier Poems.* Copyright © 1938 by New Directions Publishing Corporation. Reprinted by permission of New Directions.
"Kingdom of Mist" from *North Bank Night* by Edward Storey, by permission of the author.
"Ghosts" by Robert Service, reprinted by permission of Feinman and Krasilovsky P. C.
"The Ghost" from *Collected Poems* by Walter de la Mare. Reprinted by permission of the Literary Trustees of Walter de la Mare, and The Society of Authors as their representative.
Lilian Moore, "Teeny Tiny Ghost" (copyright © 1972 by Lilian Moore) in *See My Lovely Poison Ivy*. Copyright © 1975 by Lilian Moore. Reprinted with the permission of Atheneum Publishers.
"Haunted" from *Ghosts* by William Mayne, published by Hamish Hamilton Ltd.
"The Ghost in the Garden" from *Collected Satires and Poems* by Osbert Sitwell, published by Gerald Duckworth and Co. Ltd.
"Two's Company" from *Rhyme and Rhythm* by Raymond Wilson, reprinted by permission of Macmillan, London and Basingstoke.

"The Longest Journey in the World" by Michael Rosen, by permission of the author. First published in *A Second Poetry Book* compiled by John Foster (Oxford University Press, 1980).

Acknowledgements are also made to those few holders of copyrights whom the editor has been unable to trace in spite of careful enquiry.

Index of first lines

Index of authors